ESPECIALLY AT CHRISTMAS

CELESTINE SIBLEY

PEACHTREE PUBLISHERS, LTD.
ATLANTA, GEORGIA

Published by
PEACHTREE PUBLISHERS, LTD.
494 Armour Circle, N.E.
Atlanta, Georgia 30324

Copyright © 1985 Celestine Sibley

Previous Edition Copyright 1969

Manufactured in the United States of America

Third Printing

Library of Congress Catalog Card Number: 85-61977

ISBN 0-931948-82-7

Design by Paulette Lambert

BOOKS BY CELESTINE SIBLEY

CONTENTS

THERE'S NO SUCH THING AS A POOR CHRISTMAS

My mother, muv, once made dumplings to go with three cans of Vienna sausage for Thanksgiving dinner.

If you've ever bought Vienna sausage for seven cents a can at a sawmill-turpentine still commissary, you will understand the significance of that.

It bespeaks a woman of imagination. Who else would think the union of Vienna sausage and dumplings possible, much less feasible?

More important, it indicates an unquenchable zest for celebration.

Muv believes that you should put everything you have and everything you can get into an important occasion. We *had* the Vienna sausage — and very little else in those Depression years of the 1930's. She made the dumplings.

When I think of that Thanksgiving dinner, served out of the Sunday dishes, on the very best tablecloth, with a fire burning brightly on the hearth and a bowlful of apples our cousin sent from Virginia polished to a high sheen for a centerpiece, I wouldn't dare question Muv's convictions about Christmas.

For if Thanksgiving is important — and oh, it is! — how much more important is Christmas. Anybody who would po' mouth Christmas, contends my mother, is guilty of sinning against both heaven and his fellowman. He's a hangdog, mean-spirited character who is unworthy of receiving the greatest Gift of all time.

My father, reared a Scotch Presbyterian with a more moderate (Muv would say tepid) approach to most things, may have once regarded Muv's feelings about Christmas as a bit extravagant. But early in their marriage she beat him into line with weapons he normally handled best — ethical and spiritual arguments.

He made the mistake one grayish December morning of observing bleakly that the lumber business was going badly and "it looks like a poor Christmas this year."

"A *poor* Christmas!" cried Muv. "Shame on you! There's no such thing as a poor Christmas!"

Poor people and hard times, yes. They were not new in Christ's time and they were certainly not new in rural Alabama. But no matter what you had or didn't have in a material way, Christmas stood by itself — glorious and unmatched by anything else that had happened in the history of the world. Jesus himself had come to dwell among men, and with a richness like that to celebrate, who could be so meaching and self-centered as to speak of a "poor" Christmas?

"Make a joyful noise unto the Lord!" directed Muv gustily, and if my father found he couldn't do that, he at least didn't grouse. He was to learn later that he didn't dare to even *look* unjoyful about the approach of Christmas, or Muv would do something wild and unprecedented to cheer him up, like the year she took tailoring lessons and made him a new suit and topped it off by buying him a pearl stickpin at a $1-down-and-charge jewelry store.

The suit was beautifully made and a perfect fit and Muv had even worked out the cost of the goods by helping the tailor, but I think it made my father a little uneasy to be so splendidly arrayed at a time when he had come to accept, even to take pride in the image of himself as a "poor man." And the idea of *owing* for something as frivolous as a piece of jewelry was so repugnant to him that he finished paying for the stickpin himself. But he loved having it, wore it with pleasure, and thereafter looked at Muv and the ardor which she poured into preparations for Christmas with a touch of awe.

Things aren't important, People are, Muv preached, and it sounded so fine it was years before I realized what she meant *to us*. Things weren't important to us, so as fast as gift packages came in from distant kin, Muv unwrapped them, admired them and with a gleam in her eye that I came to dread said happily, "Now *who* can we give this to?"

It's funny that with the passage of the years only one or two of the Things stand out in memory. There were some lavender garters a boy in the sixth grade gave me. ("Beautiful!" said Muv. "You can give them to Aunt Sister!") And there was a green crepe de chine dress I think I still mourn for a little bit. ("Oh, it's so pretty! Don't you want to give it to Julia Belle?")

Julia Belle was a skinny little Negro girl in the quarters who had lost her baby in a fire and kept wandering up and down the road wringing her hands and crying. My green dress was such a dazzling gift, it did divert her from her grief a little, and it may have helped her along the road to recovery.

At the time, I remember protesting that I loved the dress and wanted it myself and Muv said blithely, "Of course you do. It's no gift if it's something you don't care about!"

It must be true because the other Things are lost to memory, but the People remain. Through the years there have been a lot of them, disreputable, distinguished, out-rageous, inspiring, and at Christmastime I remember them and the gifts they gave to me — the gifts, in fact, that they *were*.

A NEW FRIEND MAKES LIFE SO INTERESTING

MRS. RANDALL WAS THE
mother of a safecracker friend of mine. I met
him in jail. He was serving time and I was
visiting there. His name was Peewee and he
was proud of two things — his mother, and,
perhaps unwarrantedly, his ability at cracking
safes.

Once he called on me after a long silence,
during which he had been incarcerated in the

Savannah jail, and reported in tones of injury and outraged pride that the police had caught him with some burglary tools on hand and arrested him.

"You know me," he appealed. "You know I'm a *good* safecracker . . . and I couldn't have opened a can of sardines with them little old tools!"

Unswerving in her devotion to Peewee (she always called him Ernest), and her belief that he was the victim of misguided and over-zealous law enforcement officers, Mrs. Randall was a little woman of titanic spirit.

When I first went to see her, she was living in the front room of an old Victorian mansion which had been a slum for thirty years. She had just lugged a bucket of water down the winding stairs from the only bathroom in the house — a rusty assembly of plumbing that sang sibilantly in somebody else's apartment. The place was unspeakably bleak, but her room was tidy. Lacking a stove, she was cooking over a coal fire in the grate.

"Come in, my dear!" she said hospitably.

12

"Any friend of Ernest's is very welcome. Pull up that chair."

And then, pushing her stewpot to one side, "I do love an open fire, don't you?"

We spoke of trying to get Peewee a parole and she told me something of her early life in a small middle-Georgia city where her father had been a merchant and she was, as we say in the South, "raised nice." We didn't speak of her marriage or what had gone wrong in Peewee's upbringing. She talked dreamily of trips and music lessons and her indulgent father.

"My papa had my shoes handmade for me in New York," she said.

I looked at her little feet in ragged old shoes that she had tried to patch together with string, and then out at the dismal street where dirty paper blew along the sidewalk in the winter wind and some children played a game involving a beer can and broom handles.

"Oh, it must be very hard on you to have had things once, and now this . . ." I said, ready to cry.

Laughter bubbled up in the wrinkled old throat and she reached out a hand to pat my shoulder.

"Child, don't ever be discouraged, don't ever lose hope. That is the ultimate heresy. While God lives, anything can happen. Just look, here we are visiting and this morning we hadn't even met! A new friend makes life so *interesting.*"

Just before Christmas a group of us did get Peewee a parole. A day after he got home, I went by with a social worker friend to take a cot for him to sleep on. It had been heavy work, getting the old iron cot out of my garage and tying it on to the car, and we hoped that when we got to the Randalls', Peewee would take charge and unload it. Unfortunately, he had passed out cold in the middle of his mother's bed with his shoes, coat and hat on.

Outside, as we struggled up the steep front steps with the cot, I raged at the effrontery of the scrawny little safecracker to be in a drunken stupor when we were doing so much for him.

My social worker friend paused in the middle of the steps and started laughing.

"He's been working up to being what he is now for forty-five years," she said. "Do you think it's reasonable of you to expect him to change overnight just because you're giving him an old cot?"

It was a lesson that an amateur do-gooder needed badly and it has saved me from self-righteousness many a time during the years.

Mrs. Randall herself was a living lesson in optimism.

Peewee jumped his parole and was never heard from again. His mother grieved over that, but she couldn't subdue a stubborn hope that wherever he was, his horizons were expanding, he was having exciting adventures, seeing marvelous places and building a radiant new life for himself.

She went to church everyday and prayed that Ernest would give himself up and serve out his sentence. And after church she went to the library and borrowed books about San

Francisco and Canada and the Orkney Islands.

I visualized Peewee on skid row somewhere. His mother saw him as a gold miner, a whale fisherman, a Northwest Mountie or a bush pilot.

"Anything — *anything* — can happen," she assured me.

What really happened was that Peewee didn't come back and his mother moved to a meaner room in a worse slum, grew older and ill, and finally died and was buried by the county in a pauper's grave.

I think so often of her last Christmas. She had been ill a long time and her nightgown and her bedding were gray and rancid smelling. The idea of a Christmas bath for Mrs. Randall grew in my mind and, failing to find a visiting nurse who could administer it, I decided it would be my gift to her. Friends gave me some new outing-flannel nightgowns and some sheets for her and I assembled some soap and towels; and one night shortly before Christmas, I took those and a bottle of sherry to Mrs. Randall's room.

The old house was drafty and cold, and as I changed her bed, set out basin and water and spread one of the new nightgowns by the impotent little gas heater to warm, I could see that the old lady loathed the idea of a bath. She was too gracious to say so, but she abhorred the weakness and exposure and cringed at the thought of that wetness touching her shriveled old flesh.

There seemed but one thing to do and I did it. I poured out the water and opened the sherry.

We were merry as we drank it together. Her mind had been wandering for a long time but that night she was bright and lucid, asking me questions about my work and my family, listening and laughing with that special warmth and attentiveness that was hers. We got around to her own farfetched, indestructible optimism and she apparently thought about it a while.

"I may have been foolish," she remarked as I corked the sherry and closed a drawer on the new nightgowns, "but I have loved living."

Emerson was one of her favorite authors and the day of the funeral, leafing through a library book she left, I found her in something he wrote: *"To the wise life is a festival."*

It gave me a feeling that Emerson must have known Mrs. Randall as well as she knew him.

YOU ONLY HAVE WHAT YOU GIVE AWAY

OLLIE REEVES WAS ONE
of the people who worked to get Peewee a
parole and the only one to take it philosophically when he skipped town. But then Ollie
took most things philosophically.

Being a poet I guess you'd expect it of him,
except that Ollie was the most unlikely-look-
ing poet you ever saw. He was a dapper,
sports-coat and -slacks type, who had a little

clipped mustache and wore a bright feather in his tweed hat — and he owned and operated a multimillion-dollar marble-construction business, which had a part in building such things as the Lincoln Memorial in Washington and skyscrapers all over the country.

He took up writing poetry in his youth, when he was hungry and jobless, bumming around the country looking for work. Once he told me that his best work may have been done when he was sleeping on park benches in New Orleans and mooching free bananas at the fruit wharf.

"I lived for two weeks on bananas," he said. "It didn't hurt me, but it sure as hell impaired my taste for bananas."

When I met Ollie, he was a highly successful businessman whose hobby was writing a daily rhyming commentary on life and the news for the *Atlanta Constitution*. His serious poems which appeared here and there in magazines, and an occasional piece celebrating the beauty or the valorous past of the region, won him an appointment as poet laureate of Georgia. It was a title which touched and amused him. He thought a laureate should be a great deal better than he considered himself and kept suggesting people like Conrad Aiken of Savannah. But Georgians loved him and wouldn't have swapped him for Alfred Lord Tennyson or Robert Frost.

I think it was because Ollie didn't just *write* poetry. He lived it. All the old and poetic truths, which a lot of us prate because they have a fine sound, were as much a part of Ollie as the marrow in his bones:

You only have what you give away . . . When thou doest thine alms do not sound a trumpet before thee but let not thy left hand know what thy right hand doest . . . Judge not lest ye be judged.

In my work as a newspaper reporter, I was always running into cases of extreme need that couldn't be helped by any social agency, and after I had exhausted my other friends, I found Ollie remained. He never questioned, never asked if the need was legitimate or the person "worthy," never delayed. He either came himself and brought money, or he sent Joe, a bright-eyed cherubic gentleman he had sprung from jail years before and kept around his office as a sort of odd-job utility man.

Once Ollie told me if I ever ran into a person whose life could be changed for the better by "a little money," not to hesitate to call on him. He remembered his own youthful struggles and the times when a few dollars would have made a lot of difference in what he was able to accomplish. I knew he was thinking about helping a young person.

But shortly after that, the police threw Miss Lucy out of the bus station again and I called Ollie.

Miss Lucy hadn't been young since Sherman burned Atlanta. She was a fantastic-looking old lady who dyed her hair purple-black, coated her face with lavender powder and walked unceasingly around the streets of Atlanta, winter and summer, wearing deepest mourning for a sister who had died fifty years before. Her family had once been prominent in the South and she inherited a big house on a downtown street; but by the time I knew her, she had somehow lost the house and was living out of garbage cans and sleeping in doorways or at the bus station.

The proprietors at the bus station occasionally wearied of having Miss Lucy use their waiting room as a pad and the police would make her move on. They felt, justifiably, that there must be more suitable places and that the county welfare could surely do something. But they didn't understand Miss Lucy. She wouldn't accept an old-age pension. She wasn't that old, she said, and besides her family had never found it necessary to "receive charity." In vain, I pointed out that they had been proud taxpayers for more than a century and she would only be getting back some of her own money.

Miss Lucy was adamant and I would have washed my hands of her, but a storm came up the night she was last ousted from the bus station, and when I saw her, she was soaked to the skin and had a deep, hacking cough.

I called Ollie and reminded him what he had said about changing lives. I didn't mention that the person was old and the change would be only a matter of a roof over her head, as opposed to no roof. He didn't ask, he just sent the money. I gave it to Miss Lucy in weekly installments, and I got her to take it by telling her that it came from a man who was greatly indebted to her sainted father.

It was exactly the kind of thing she would have expected of her papa, she said. He was "a very elegant gentleman," who was very kind to common people and would be pleased to know that gratitude existed among the lower classes.

Miss Lucy had been living in relative comfort for a couple of years before I confessed to Ollie what I was doing with his money. One day, his visit to the office to drop off a sheaf of his "Rhyme A Day" columns happened to coincide with Miss Lucy's call to pick up her rent money. She looked exactly like a moth-eaten old bird that had been blown out of a taxidermist's window — black dress, man's

gray fedora hat, chewed-up old fur coat and a
crutch which she didn't lean on but swung
like a swagger stick.

She picked her way daintily through what
she considered a coarse assemblage of people
in the newsroom until she reached my desk
and collected her money. I watched her pro-
gress toward the elevator and on an impulse I
pointed her out to Ollie.

"See her?" I said. "She's the girl whose rent
you've been paying."

Ollie choked on some popcorn he was
eating.

"I'll be damned!" he said.

When he recovered from the shock of that,
I described to him his role as a grateful peasant who had once benefited from her elegant
papa's largesse.

Ollie handed me the rest of the popcorn
and laughed until he steamed up his bifocals.

"I'm a peasant, all right," he said, "and if
her old man had been around I would proba-
bly have *tried* to borrow money from him."

And then he noted worriedly that Miss

Lucy looked thin and scrawny and he gave me some more money to make sure she had groceries each week.

When Miss Lucy died a few years later, two of her nieces blew into town to claim her estate, which, surprisingly enough, turned out to include some other property. They were dreadful women who were ashamed of "Awnt Lucy" and kept telling me, "We girls really didn't *know* Awnt Lucy." I took a nasty pleasure in noting that even as they floundered around in their disclaimers they bore a marked resemblance to "Awnt Lucy" with their dyed hair and powdery faces. But their fur coats were new.

I hated for them to get what the little old lady had forgotten owning. I urged Ollie to come forward and put in a bid for the years' support he had given her, but he wouldn't. What he had done for her had enriched him, he said, and to scrabble over her estate, even if it had been worth a million dollars, would only diminish his gift.

Ollie believed that and lived by it, just as he

took no credit for helping Peewee, and did not rail and complain and grow cynical when Peewee violated his parole.

Peewee, I found out, was one of scores of convicts Ollie helped. He traveled thousands of miles to appear before parole boards and get freedom for federal prisoners that he met while teaching a class at Atlanta Penitentiary and believed deserved a chance. He found them jobs and staked them to clothes and a place to live, even buying one man who wanted to be a novelist, a new typewriter. Many of them fulfilled his belief in them and became useful, law-abiding citizens. Some, mostly the ones I sent him, skipped out, eventually landing back in jail.

Ollie didn't take credit for the good ones or feel abused by the bad ones.

"You do what you can to help when you see the need," he said simply. "What happens then is up to the Lord."

CHRISTMAS NIGHT ... AND ALL THE OTHERS

IN MANY WAYS
I suspect my friend, Mrs. Arizona Bell, was a palpable old fraud — but not where it counted.

She claimed to be in her nineties and I wouldn't have doubted it, because on a bitter-cold night when she got herself together to sell papers down at the corner of Broad and Walton streets, she might have been as old as anything unearthed from an Egyptian tomb. She wore a World War I army coat, which hit her shoetops (also GI issue), a streetcar motorman's gloves and a Red Grange type football helmet. (This last caused a whole generation of Atlanta children to call her "Halfback.")

The only reason I doubted that she was ninety-odd instead of a mere eighty-odd was that she showed me some newspaper clippings about her "walking feats" in the West when she was a girl, and every date and every reference to her age had been carefully punched out.

She also told me that she was a twin.

"I was named Arizona and my brother was named California," she related. "He busted his brains out riding Roman style around the hippodrome in Buffalo Bill's circus."

And in the middle of the sidewalk she would demonstrate Roman style — one foot on one horse, one on another.

She herself had progressed from the circus to play in stock, she said. She professed to know Mary Pickford and her mother well.

"Little Mary died in my arms on the stage every night for three months while we toured the West," she said proudly.

But when Mary Pickford came to town and I went to interview her, she couldn't quite place Mrs. Bell. And Mrs. Bell was nowhere to be found, although I tried to set up a reunion.

"I took sick," she told me brusquely, when I questioned her about it at her stand on the corner that night.

There was the matter of her husbands. She claimed to have been married six or seven times, but when I got interested in tracking down some of her husbands with the hope of finding some money for her, she dismissed them all as "dead — long dead."

"What happened to Ed?" I persisted.

"Married him on Tuesday, buried him on Thursday," she said briefly.

"And George?"

Mrs. Bell's taste for theatrics came to her rescue, her eyes brightened and she reared back to tell a story, the gist of which was that a terrible fate befell George.

"Found him floating in the river," she said with doleful satisfaction. "His feet was in the Mississippi, his head in the Ohio."

Husbands or no husbands, Mrs. Bell was good company and a lot of us enjoyed taking time to visit with her at the bus stop on our way home at night. She was proud of the fact that one of her credit customers was Atlanta's mayor for a quarter of a century, William B. Hartsfield. He would stop by his law office on his way home from the city hall at night and, frequently, wouldn't have a nickel to pay for his *Constitution* when he was ready to board the bus.

He not only was a good credit risk, Mrs. Bell felt, but such a good mayor that when he had opposition one term, she broke a habit of a lifetime and registered so she could vote for him. She hadn't thought it quite "nice" for a lady to vote, she confided, but there were times when the need for bold action overbalanced decorum. Once she had voted, Mrs.

Bell found it such a heady experience, she joined the League of Women Voters and really got interested in politics.

One time I dressed Mrs. Bell up and took her to opening night at the Metropolitan Opera. She was so pleased that I didn't even have to be ashamed that I was impelled to do it for a story.

"Grand opera!" she exulted. "I'd *love* to go! You know I was in show business once myself."

We borrowed some finery from one of Atlanta's well-to-do matrons, who got into the spirit of the thing and sent a corsage to go with it. We did the hairdresser and the manicurist and the chiropodist and even hired a car and driver, so she could arrive in style. The only thing that detracted from Mrs. Bell's pleasure was that I had been so intent on the story, I went wearing the same wrinkled linen dress I'd been in all day.

She surveyed her glittering image in the mirror at the theater and then looked at me.

"Dear, you really should try to fix yourself

up a little," she murmured.

And it scandalized her that the star of the performance, Marguerite Piazza, was several months pregnant, a state which was fairly obvious when she was onstage and which was discussed freely in the press.

"In my day," said Mrs. Bell severely, "a woman wouldn't even have gone out of the house in that condition."

In her own odd way, Mrs. Bell was as active as the Community Chest in helping people. Willie Jones, an old wino who would sell papers until he had the price of a drink and then desert his post and head for the Rose Tap Room, was scorned by most of the street sales fraternity as a no-good stumblebum. He was a wretched fellow and the nearest thing he had to a home was the drunk tank at the jail. When he was out, he slept in doorways or the gutter until the police found him and took him in again.

When Mrs. Bell found out about it, she took her fellow newsies to task.

"He's a human being!" she cried. "Ain't we

all human too?"

She gave the men in the group such a tongue-lashing, some of them took Willie home with them for a meal and a bath. Mrs. Bell took him to church with her and had him drop by her immaculate little housekeeping room on Sunday afternoon for coffee, her celebrated floating island pudding and conversation. Somehow, prodded and shamed by Mrs. Bell, the newsies closed ranks around Willie, helping him sell his papers when the weather was bad and his thirst was worse, bringing him hot coffee and sandwiches and including him in their jokes and their sociability.

I'd like to say such care transformed Willie into a sober, upright citizen. All I know is that he was out of jail for a long stretch and he looked better. But then he died.

The cancer from which he had been suffering for a long time, took him one night as he slept on a cot in the room of one of his new friends.

Mrs. Bell was comforted that he "died

respectable and looked after" and she took up a collection to buy him a funeral.

"We put him away nice," she told me the night after the obsequies. And then, shifting her papers about on their applebox stand, she said a thing I have never forgotten.

"Ain't it hard," she asked sadly, "for us human beings to *be* human?"

Although I knew Mrs. Bell was popular, I may have attributed it to the fact that she was a sort of minor celebrity in our town and I was her self-appointed press agent. I didn't realize how valiantly she did her small job in life, what care and creativity she brought to a very humble calling.

Christmas night is always an anti-climax. The festivities are over. Everybody is celebrated out and ready to stay home and fall into bed early. On such a night, somebody called to tell me that Mrs. Bell was ill on the street corner where she worked. I said I could call Grady Hospital right away.

"It won't do any good," the voice said. "They sent an ambulance already, but she won't go. She says she's going to sell her papers. I'm afraid it's pneumonia."

It was pneumonia, but Mrs. Bell would not give up and go to the hospital until some friends and I promised to take over her corner and stay there and sell her papers until the last bus had run at 2 A.M.

"I got to see after my customers," she insisted. "It's a bad night and they're tired and cold and they expect me to be here with their paper. My boys on the buses . . ."

A fit of coughing seized her and she pointed to a Thermos jug she had brought to town. It was full of hot coffee for her "boys," the bus drivers. She knew that the restaurants where they normally stopped would be closed, that the passengers would be few and the runs long and lonesome, and she had brought them coffee.

A lot of people who remember Arizona Bell think her finest hour was the Fourth of July when on her ninety-eighth birthday (she said), she dived from the high board at Grant Park. But to me it will always be the icy

winter nights, that Christmas night and all
the others, when she stood on her corner —
selling her papers, joking with lonely, tired
people, giving her "boys" a cup of coffee —
fulfilling some private, personal high stan-
dard of job performance.

THE BEST
CHRISTMAS

You couldn't really call Mrs. Dooley a spiritual type but she takes such pleasure in living, has such a fine earthy acceptance of life as it is, that it cheers me to think of her.

The day I met her she was being evicted from a room where she lived with three babies — triplets — that she had given birth to a month before.

"We gon' be set out on the street and hit a-raining," she told me.

I suggested that a story about her plight and pictures of the triplets in our newspaper might help to find her housing. She was willing.

"I sure hope so," she said. "The Carnation Milk and the Tidy-Didy is a-giving the 'trips' milk and diapers and with all them cans of milk and all them diapers a-piling up, we need to situate in a hurry."

The day the pictures and the story appeared in the paper, offers of housing did indeed come pouring in and I got a staff car and went by to pick up Mrs. Dooley and the triplets, to inspect what was offered. By the time I got there, Mrs. Dooley had been to the Methodist and Baptist orphanages and got out her other six children that she had stashed away, so we had *nine* children instead of three to find housing for.

One of the first places we went to was out the Marietta highway to Happy Hooligan's barbecue stand. Happy, the most doleful-

looking character I ever saw, had a room back
of his establishment which he said Mrs.
Dooley could use. And then, his eyes resting
on the six big children, he suggested that they
could serve as carhops to work out the rent.

"I just purely love chil'ren," he said. "I
ain't never had none. My wife's been pary-
lized from the waist down for twenty year."

It was then I noticed that Mrs. Dooley was
a rather handsome woman except for one
slight idiosyncracy. In moments of emotional
stress or excitement, her eyes would cross.
They crossed at Happy's suggestion and with
a rush of sympathy she cried: "Good man, I
know just what you're up against! You and
me can help one another!"

I hated to be a killjoy, but I couldn't see ten
people living in that one room, even if three of
them were babies and six of them were carhops. So I dragged Mrs. Dooley and her
brood away and eventually got them
ensconced in a neat, warm apartment in a
Federal Housing Project. I was proud of that
place. It had good plumbing and sunny

clotheslines and an enclosed playground for the children. But Mrs. Dooley hated it and after a month she left it and took her nine children and moved back to the slums — to two rooms.

"You know how it is with them federals," she told me. "They rule and regerlate the life out of you."

While Mrs. Dooley and I had traveled around looking at apartments, we became pretty good friends and she told me the story of her life and of her marriage to the late Hampton P. Dooley. He pushed an ice-cream hunky cart for a living and instead of ringing a little bell to alert the customers to his approach, he would honk like a southbound goose. So they called him Gander Dooley.

He was "a sweet thang," Mrs. Dooley said. "Polite and nice as you ever saw." But he had one little old failing. Every time she was expecting a baby, he would disappear.

She didn't hold it against him. "You seen delicate people, ain't you?" she asked.

It was a delicacy unfortunate in the father of

nine children, I said, and she told me she thought so too. She had made up her mind once to break him of it, she said.

"It was after Buddy was borned and we was a-living down yonder on Pulliam Street. Mr. Dooley he come a-wavering back a-looking sheepylike and I said, 'Mr. Dooley, you got the leaving habit, you just as well to leave now as . . . *later.*'"

Mr. Dooley said, "Aw, Birdie Lou, you know you don't want me to go. The buggers'll git you."

But Mrs. Dooley was firm. She said, "Buggers or no buggers, you go on down the road, sir."

So Mr. Dooley left and, as she related, "I went in the house to git up a washing of clothes I was a-doing for a neighbor. I opened the closet door and there was quiled up on them clothes the biggest snake ever you seen! I yelled to the young'uns to run git the hoe and they couldn't find the hoe so they got . . . Mr. Dooley."

After that the triplets were conceived —

and Mr. Dooley died.

Mrs. Dooley seemed to think it was appropriate for him to disappear permanently before so phenomenal a birth as the triplets.

"I often wonder what he would have thought" she mused, "him being a man in his seventies like he was."

When Mrs. Dooley moved from the housing project back to the slums she took in a gentleman lodger. By that time we were fast friends, and all of the people who had helped Mrs. Dooley in one way or another started urging me to speak to her about the impropriety of having a man in the house. Like the late Mr. Dooley I felt a certain delicacy, but one day I summoned my courage and mentioned it to Mrs. Dooley.

"You know the teachers who gave the triplets the coats . . ." I began.

"Evva one of 'em *different!*" cried Mrs. Dooley. "For triplets, mind you, and evva one of them coats different!"

I apologized for that and lumbered on. The teachers didn't think it was quite *suitable* for her to have a gentleman lodger.

"That's the way it goes," said Mrs. Dooley, sighing. "Folks hep you and they want to run your business."

The public health nurses, I persisted, didn't think it was quite *sanitary,* all of them being there *together.*

"Them old maids!" said Mrs. Dooley scornfully. "Don't they know love is the healthiest thing they is?"

After that I felt a little coolness between Mrs. Dooley and me. She seemed to have put me in a class with schoolteachers, public health nurses, "them welfares," "them juveniles" and others of the stripe and we just weren't as close as we had once been. I missed her, too, because she is a real philosopher and in times past I had enjoyed calls from her.

"You know," she would say in some weighty discussion of life and its vicissitudes, "if it ain't the physical, it's the mental and if it ain't the mental, it's the *fi*-nancial . . . all the time."

Whether pressure of public opinion had

anything to do with it, I don't know, but Mrs. Dooley later married the lodger and right away called up with the news. When I congratulated her she said, "Well, I thank you. It *is* nice. I like him and the chil'ren they like him too. But . . ." dropping her voice confidentially, "he ain't a-working."

He had quit his job in the cotton mill to take them all on a honeymoon to "Chattanoogy" and when they returned "them welfares," seeing a legal man in the house, had cut them off the Aid to Dependent Children program.

"And we gon' be set out on the street and hit a-raining again," concluded the bride.

I started to sympathize with her, but she was laughing and I knew the old hearty, ebullient spirit was not cast down. She said all she wanted me to do was to help them get jobs.

"You take charity," she said, "it ain't reliable nohow."

The marriage, I regret to say, was short-lived. The bridegroom took a powder and Mrs. Dooley grieved for a time. The privations of her second widowhood upset her so, she called one day and urged me to write a story exposing Grady Hospital. People down there, she said, were putting Spanish fly in her snuff.

"You being a lady your ownself," she pointed out, "you know they ain't a one of us that can withstand that stuff."

From time to time she would need help in making a payment on "the teevee" just before the sheriff came to repossess it. She was finally reconciled to living in a housing project and it was there a few years ago that she really proved her mettle.

Christmas came and for once in all the years she had put up with them welfares, them juveniles, church ladies and assorted do-gooders, Mrs. Dooley struck it rich. Their system of checks and balances broke down. Never before in her long association with them had she witnessed what they abhorred above all — duplication of services.

"Lord God, hit's Kingdom Come!" she told me ecstatically. "Pore baskets are pouring in here a mile a minute! We got three turkeys and two hams and more fatback than you can shake a stick at. Theys cakes and oranges and apples and pecans and Tootsie Rolls that won't wait. I want you to come see; we're plumb wallering in plenty!"

I had a fleeting feeling that I should call somebody, but I didn't get around to it and I'm glad because the day after Christmas Mrs. Dooley gave me a report on the disposition of her goodies. She and the children had repacked the baskets and gone abroad into the housing project and their old neighborhood and given to everybody who needed. The turkeys and the hams and the fruits and candies went first and after that they gave out the fatback and the collard greens and all the canned goods.

"Never had such a good time in my life," she said happily, "and you shoulda seen how the chil'ren enjoyed it."

"What did you keep for them?" I asked.

"Two cans of chicken soup," she said.

I started to remonstrate with her but she

interrupted me to say something which will always stay in my mind as a poignant statement of Christmas.

"Don't you say a word, good woman," she said with dignity. "My chil'ren have been receiving and receiving all their lives. This is the best Christmas they ever had. Nobody ought to be so pore they can't ever *give* at Christmastime."

A TRULY CONTENTED WOMAN

CONTENTMENT MUST BE one of fortune's greatest gifts. I don't know if it is something one is born with, or if it can be achieved. But when I think of Miss Lovie Keener, I at least make an effort to *see* what I have and to value it.

Miss Lovie lived in a remote cove in the mountains of north Georgia, in a little cabin which her grandfather built when he came over the gap from "Ca'lina" in a "kivvered wagon." She lived pretty much as her grandparents and her parents had lived, drawing her water from a spring in a cleft in the hill, raising her food and cooking it in iron pots on trivets in the great stone fireplace.

She was a patrician-looking old lady, then eighty-six years old with snow-white hair, flawless teeth and bright-blue eyes. She wore a dress which she had made by hand from wool sheared from her own sheep, hand-carded and -spun, woven on her grandmother's old loom and dyed with walnut hulls.

Our mountain friend, Herbert Tabor, took Bill Young, a photographer, and me by Miss Lovie's when we were headed somewhere back in the mountains on a story about something else. She couldn't have been more gracious. She invited us to come in and offered us a drink of water from her spring.

"Hit's a good spring of water," she said proudly. "Would you'uns like to see it?"

It was a beautiful spring, flowing from a

ferny bank at the foot of a giant beech tree.
Bloodroot and hepatica grew up the bank and
Miss Lovie pointed these out along with the
heartleaves and wild ginger. As we dipped the
cold, sweet water from the spring she
watched us expectantly and accepted our
praise with pleasure.

She showed us the fine shade trees which
sheltered her cabin and the view from the
mountains from the little porch which she
called "the front shed."

Electric lines ran into her cabin but I didn't
see any lights and I asked her if she used
electricity.

"Bless you, no," she said laughing. "That's
here because the people in the settlement
beyan' the gap needed one more name on the
list to get the rural electric to come in. I ain't
never needed hit. I go to bed by dark. Why I
got lamp ile I ain't used!"

The way she said it — lamp "ile" more than
sufficient for her needs — sounded like abun-
dance heaped up, pressed down and running
over. What more could any woman want than

lamp ile she ain't used?

When she learned that we had come from Atlanta, Miss Lovie's face was alive with interest. Although the state capital was less than a hundred miles away, she had never been there and she wanted us to tell her about it.

"Tell me hit's mighty nigh ten miles acrost hit," she said.

We told her all we could think to tell her of the state's biggest city — the tall buildings with elevators in them, the railroads that crisscrossed it, the jetliners that landed there from all parts of the world. She listened eagerly, asking questions from time to time and catching her breath at our talk of big stores with moving stairs.

Then I said, "Miss Lovie, we'd love to take you to Atlanta if you'd care to go. We'll come back for you any day you say."

She laughed and shook her head.

"No, I'm much obliged," she said, "but hit's too fur to walk and cars jiggle you so bad."

As we were leaving I noticed a pile of fire-wood by her door and I asked her how she got it. Some neighbors hauled logs from the woods for her, she said, "and I work hit up myself."

"What do you mean you 'work it up'?" asked Bill Young, the photographer.

"Why, I saw hit," she said.

"Do you mind if I get a picture of that?" asked Bill.

Miss Lovie smiled tolerantly and picked up an old but well-sharpened saw and sent its teeth singing into a hard white-oak log. Amusement at Bill, whose Boston accent had already attracted her, finally caused her to stop sawing and give way to laughter.

"Ain't you ever seed nobody saw wood before?" she asked.

"Yes, ma'am," said Bill, "but they weren't ladies in their eighties."

That was even funnier to Miss Lovie. A lady in her eighties had to have firewood the same as anybody else, didn't she? She gloried in the fact that her land offered plenty of wood and that she had the strength to "work it up."

Miss Lovie was one of the few truly contented women I have known and it wasn't a blind, passive, do-nothing contentment. She knew there was a different, easier life "beyan'" the hills, but she saw and knew for its true worth the life she had, the peace and the beauty, the fine shade trees and the matchless "spring of water," the satisfying work, the independence.

When Miss Lovie died and her relations came across the mountain to close up her house, they found under a loose stone on her hearth all the Old-Age Assistance checks she had ever received. Miss Lovie hadn't much need for money.

"I reckon she was saving them for her old age," a niece observed.

Old age never overtook Miss Lovie.

THE
CHRISTMAS
DOLLHOUSE

SPRING WAS REALLY
Ruth Sefton's time of year. When the sun lay
gently on the red earth of Georgia and the
silver buds on the dogwood trees were ready
to explode into bloom, she would look out
the window, rubbing the scarred half-hand
where she had lost some fingers, and her eyes
would grow bright and dreamy.

"Ought to be rolling . . . rolling," she

would murmur.

And then she would talk of the old days when she was a snake charmer in a carnival and how it was in the spring when the shows would come out of winter hibernation and take to the road. They were wagon shows in those days, traveling dirt roads, and it was a blessing to be out there with them, seeing life come back to the earth and the winterlocked little towns moving and stirring.

Gripped by vernal restlessness she would gather up the neighborhood children and walk them to the city zoo, calling it a hike so they wouldn't mind not having carfare. Or she would stride down the back alleys of the shabby old street where she lived, looking for fugitive plants she could pot for her windowsill, or coax back to health in the small yards of friends she visited.

"You'd be surprised how stubborn beauty is," she would say. "It *wants* to live."

All kinds of horticultural surprises turned up in the rubbish piles of the alley — bulbs that were thrown out years ago when paid gardeners tended the yards of the old houses, sprigs of verbena and tendrils of clematis and yellow jasmine, Johnny-jump-ups and Wandering Jew, Job's-tears and liriope.

Mrs. Sefton knew them all, and trowel in hand, rejoiced over each acquisition. She had little space for them in her one room, but she could place them handily with friends. There was an old country couple down the street, brought to town by their children who sold their farm and put them in a little apartment to live out the rest of their days, with only a window-sized patch of sour city soil and part of a tree to refresh their eyes and spirit. Mrs. Sefton enticed them out-of-doors with gifts of plants and tales of rich dirt up the alley, free for the taking.

She worked beside them, telling wondrous stories of phenomenal tomato plants growing refulgently in tubs and barrels, and bean vines trained on fences, until the old couple forgot their lost country acres and became what she called contented "tin-can gardeners."

She picked seed pods off shrubs in the

parks and any front yard where she could reach them from the sidewalk, and set them in pots to "see what they will do." Somehow, the excitement and suspense of even this limited gardening was transmitted to a lot of young couples and to children who otherwise might never have seen the little question mark of a bean sprout break ground, or the diminutive Christmas tree a pine seedling makes.

But it was to one particular old "carnie" friend that Mrs. Sefton brought most of her gifts of plants and gardening know-how. She met Flossie when she herself was "working snakes" and Flossie and her husband ran a ringtoss game.

They weren't prosperous then, but they were young and their husbands were living and Flossie, "as pretty as a fistful of cotton candy," dreamed of fame and fortune.

"She thought Ziegfeld was going to discover her and we all hoped he would, because she would have shared anything she had with us all. Me and John were having lean times. Snakes weren't hot that year and we had put all our savings into a boa constrictor to try and pep up the act. We nearly went broke feeding him. They have to have live food, you know, and we'd buy chickens for that snake and stand by with our stomachs growling and watch him eat 'em, feathers and all."

It was that year a rattler bit Ruth and caused her to lose half her hand. She was standing on the platform in front of the tent with the rattlesnake draped over her shoulders, while her husband John gave the spiel about the show.

"My John, being an Irishman, could never talk without waving his hands. I saw the movement was attracting the snake's attention. I put up my hand to turn his head away from John and he struck me."

They had no money when they got to the nearest hospital, and while they waited for carnival friends to arrive with funds, the venom moved swiftly, with the result that Ruth lost her thumb and two fingers from her right hand.

She wasn't bitter about it. Small town

people in those days were suspicious of "carnies" and the doctor had great contempt for anybody who would fool around with rattlesnakes.

"I never faulted him for it," she said. "I didn't really like snakes myself. I got into the act because John had it when I married him. Never knew why the Bible speaks of the 'wisdom' of a serpent. I thought they were plumb stupid."

Flossie and her husband had it a little better. Small town and country people liked what Ruth called the "chicken gambling" of the ringtoss game and were willing to spend a dime any day with the hope of winning an orange-glass bonbon dish, or a Kewpie Doll in a crepe-paper skirt. It wasn't until Flossie was old and her husband was dead that she returned to a little country house on the outskirts of Atlanta which her farmer father left her.

It seemed sheer riches to Mrs. Sefton, also widowed, that old frame house with a bit of land around it. But Flossie, finally facing the knowledge that Ziegfeld wasn't going to discover her, "turned scared." She had nothing, after a while, but the house and a little welfare check, and, frightened over what the future might hold, she became a compulsive eater, stuffing herself until she split out of her clothes and overflowed her chair.

Mrs. Sefton visited her often, trying to keep up her interest in gardening, dressing herself up in some of John's old clothes and posing as a yardman so Flossie would feel free to boss her around and regain some of her old sense of affluence. Flossie took pleasure in the yard and plants as long as she had her "pretend" yardman there to order about, but when Ruth left she would retreat to the pantry and gobble up her month's grocery supply.

Toward the last she began to see herself as a little girl bereft of all who loved and sheltered her and she dragged her fat, arthritic old body around the house, weeping inconsolably and throwing shrill, childlike tantrums until the neighbors complained and county officials talked of having her committed to the state mental hospital.

The year things got so bad with Flossie, Mrs. Sefton called and asked me to drive her out to visit her friend and take her a Christmas present. Ruth was ruggedly independent and either rode the bus or walked everywhere she wanted to go and I was surprised at her request until I saw the present.

It was a dollhouse made of crates and apple boxes from the grocery store and completely furnished, down to pots and pans and food on the shelf and a family of tiny wooden dolls with painted faces.

Awkwardly, because of her hand, Mrs. Sefton had worked for months to build it, hammering the house together, gluing the furniture and carving the dolls with an old pocketknife. The little chairs were a work of art, copies of country rockers with hand-woven cane seats. And because she was good at weaving them, there were tiny baskets all over the house — clothes and picnic hampers and an infinitesimal sewing basket with a pincushion no bigger than a peanut. She had made curtains and rich velvet portieres for the doors from scraps, and quilts and pillows for the little beds.

As touching as her devotion to her friend was, it seemed to me to be a terrible expenditure of time and energy for a loony old woman. I worried all the way out to the country that Flossie might scorn the gift and wreck it with one sweeping whack.

Mrs. Sefton knew her need better than I did.

"Let's go in singing," she directed as we stopped in the dirt drive before the old house.

We stepped out into the bright frosty sunshine, lugging the dollhouse between us, puffing and singing off-key, "Deck the halls with boughs of holly!" until Flossie came to the door.

She came, sliding her feet along in men's old slippers, pulling a grease-spotted chenille robe around her, her eyes swollen and red-rimmed from crying.

She had drawn the shades and turned up

her heaters full blast and it was dark and hot in the house. When she saw Ruth, she started whimpering and holding out her arms in the gesture of a child who wants to be picked up.

"Oh, Floss," said Ruth gently, putting her arms around the mammoth shoulders and hugging her. "Run fix your face, you look a sight. Get your lipstick. Where's your mascara? My God, suppose Flo Ziegfeld walked in now!"

Flossie giggled and shuffled off and Ruth turned down heaters and raised the shades to let the sunshine pour into the rooms. There was a row of dirty dishes by the bed and she picked them up and took them to the kitchen, whistling a Christmas carol as she worked.

Flossie didn't notice the dollhouse until she returned. We had set it on a little table by the window and Ruth was straightening the furniture when Flossie came in, her hair combed, her old mouth smeared with magenta, a dragon-embroidered Chinese robe a little more than half-covering her night clothes.

Ruth smiled and held out the little wooden girl-child to her and, with a swift intake of breath, Flossie reached for it.

"Oh, Ruth," she said softly. "Oh, look."

She hunched over the table and gently touched the tiny windows with the holly wreaths in them. She moved a little rocker and picked up the mother and father dolls and held them against her cheek. The small pantry with its modelling-clay vegetables and round loaves of bread attracted her and she ran a finger along the shelf, straightening the food, pushing the little dishes back from the edge.

When I left, the old lady had moved a chair to the window by the table, and her puffy old hands moved with surprising lightness and grace through the miniature rooms as she crooned softly to her new family.

Mrs. Sefton stayed to make a pot of coffee and visit a while, but she followed me to the car when I left.

"I need a bit of pine," she said, looking about the yard. "Flossie wants to make a little Christmas tree for the dolls."

THE MAN WHO WROTE CHRISTMAS BALLADS

ALMOST EVERY CHRISTMAS
among the cards that come, there will be one
showing a little child in a ragged coat walking
along a lonesome road. The verse is brief and
different:

> "If I but had a little coat,
>   A coat to fit a no-year-old,
>   I'd button it close about His throat

> To cover Him from the cold.
>   The cold,
> To cover Him from the cold."

There's more to the poem, although it's not on the card. Like an old mountain ballad it runs on for many verses, and the last three are:

> "If I had a little shoe,
>   A little shoe as might be found
>   I'd lace it on with a sheepskin thew
> To keep His foot from the ground,
>   The ground,
> To keep His foot from the ground.
>
> If my heart were a shining coin,
>   A silver coin or a coin of gold
>   Out of my side I'd it purloin
> And give it to Him to hold,
>   To hold,
> And give it to Him to hold.
>
> If my heart were a house also,

A house also with room to spare
I never would suffer my Lord to go
Homeless, but house Him there,
    O there,
*Homeless, but house Him there!"**

It sings of Christmas to me as much as any
carol, and I think of the young man who wrote
it and how simple and personal the wonder of
the Christmas story became in his telling.

He wrote of Mary as if she were a young
mountain girl any of us might know:

"In Nazareth dwelt Mary mild,
   She carded and she spun;
   On Christmas Day she bore the child
   Of God, His Holy Son."

He wrote of the Christmas search of the
shepherds, hearing a cry in the night:

* "Adoration" from *Bow Down in Jericho*, E. P. Dutton & Co. 1950

> *"If not a lamb what is it cries*
> *Unhousen in the waste,"*

He retold the legend of the fir tree that went to Bethlehem to "see the Christ child good" and Mary's foreboding:

> *"She said, Thy trunk is big about,*
> *Shades in thy branches brood,*
> *Forsooth, but thou art dark and stout*
> *Enough to make a rood!"**

Byron Herbert Reece was a Georgia mountain farmer whose poetry was discovered back in the 1940's by another mountaineer, Kentucky's Jesse Stuart. His verses had appeared here and there in the kind of little magazine that had a "discontinued" after its name by the time he was persuaded to assem-

---

* "Mary" from *Bow Down in Jericho*, E. P. Dutton & Co. 1950
"The Shepherds in Search of the Lamb of God" *Ibid.*
"The Pilgrim and the Fir Tree" *Ibid.*

ble enough of them for a book. And most of us had never heard of either young Mr. Reece or his work until "Ballad of the Bones" was published in 1945.

He stayed at home in the little slant-roofed house his parents owned on Wolf Creek in the shadow of Blood Mountain; plowing and planting and hauling wood and moving rocks; feeding stock and milking cows and writing late at night.

When his first novel, *Better a Dinner of Herbs,* was accepted his publishers thought they would telephone Byron, and I guess there was some amusement in New York literary circles when they found they had to call the little town of Blairsville and send word to Choestoe district "by first passing." The Reeces had no telephone, nor did any other mountain family in similar circumstances. It could have been hours or days before Byron got the message and was able to put down what he was doing and get into the county seat to return the call.

He would have liked conveniences. There

were even certain luxuries that he coveted sometimes. He told me once that he longed for a good high-fidelity record player and all the music he could hear. And at the same time he laughingly confessed that feeding and milking cows was a chore "so regular," he'd be glad to see the day when Wolf Creek was on some dairy's milk route.

But he loved the land and the wildness and loneliness of the mountains. The first time I ever heard from him was when I wrote of the desolation of Blood Mountain, comparing it unfavorably, I'm afraid, to the settled valleys of Rabun Gap where there were friendly chimneys and church steeples to be seen, and cowbells and dogs barking to be heard at dusk. He took me to task for holding a narrow, womanish view and after I apologized properly we were friends.

I went to a party his neighbors and friends had for him when he returned to the hill country after a trip to New York to accept a Guggenheim Fellowship and to be lionized at literary parties. Tall, gaunt, weather-roughened, he looked like a young Lincoln, or, as Frank Daniel, another newspaper friend once observed, a young and unfrightened Ichabod Crane. Shy and awkward-looking he had the quiet man's poise, the mountain man's humor — and he enjoyed the jokes on city jumpers-to-conclusions.

There was the writer who was interested that his father, a Georgia farmer descended from Georgia farmers, should have a Spanish name, Juan.

"Wan?" Byron repeated it, laughing. "At home we call that Joo-ann."

Another writer, noting the unmistakable Elizabethan flavor of some of his poems, assumed that he had been named Byron for the English poet.

The night of the party, he took delight in hearing old friends tell how it really was. Herbert Tabor, the Ellijay insurance man, was at the gathering and he told of driving into the Reeces' yard after a hazardous trip over the unpaved mountain roads in a Model-T Ford one day in 1918.

"Juan greeted me in the yard with the news that they had a new baby, born the night before," Mr. Tabor related. "Since I was its first visitor, they were going to name the little chap for me and for Byron Watkins, the best butcher in Union County."

"*Lord* Byron, ha!" Byron Herbert jeered delightedly.

Byron grew up in a house where they had a great respect for learning, but few books. Like most rural Southerners they had a Bible and a copy of Shakespeare's works and Byron read both, nearly every day of his life. Later when he was a teacher, lecturing at colleges around the country, he liked to point out the way the language of the southern highlands, commonly supposed to be illiterate, really sprang from such highly thought of poets as Milton, Spenser and even Lovelace.

"A few years ago," he once wrote, "only teachers, lawyers and preachers spoke English. The rest of us spoke Anglish, pure and simple."

There was a flavor of "Anglish" in his own slow speech when he spoke of rutted, weather-pocked roads as "gouted," a sturdy, well-built house as a "lasty" house and good bottom land as "yieldy" land. He was educated beyond the local custom of adding "es" to make plurals of most words — "postes, costes, beastes" — but, to him, the fearful were sometimes "acowered" and the gossip-monger "gathered sketches."

Tuberculosis, for some reason, used to strike the homes of mountaineers more often than those in the lowlands and Byron and several members of his family were plagued by it. He was the mainstay of his parents and a younger sister, and when tuberculosis hit him, he tried to stay out of a sanitarium by building himself a little one-room isolation house in the yard. He hated the imprisonment of a hospital, and it might have been the prospect of unending illness and hospitalization which caused him to take his own life one night of June 1958 when he was in temporary residence as a lecturer at Young Harris College, the little mountain school not many miles from his home.

For many years it was the fashion among his writing — and reading — friends to deplore the fact that Byron had to work so hard tilling the rocky mountain acres. They deplored the waste of his time and strength, and when one friend heard that he was plowing potatoes instead of writing, she scolded him, saying, *"Anybody* can plow potatoes."

"Anybody *can* plow potatoes," Byron said lightly, "but nobody is willing to plow mine but me."

He may have regretted the harsh demands of farming sometimes. Once he wrote in the Sunday *Atlanta Journal* Magazine, "As a pair, farming and writing are like two crippled men who have only one good pair of hands between them. Still, with its one good hand each helps the other."

Although he himself produced five books and corn "sufficient to bread us" and innumerable crops of hay, potatoes and vegetables before his death at the age of forty, he was ever-mindful that for the farmer-writer, "a combination of droughts and dubious editors could very easily add up to starvation."

Once, I was presumptuous enough to sympathize with him over having a family to support. He was in town to autograph one of his books and he talked eagerly of a trilogy he wanted to write and the pleasures of travel and meeting other writers. It seemed unfair that he, of all people, had to bog himself down in farm chores and the care of old parents.

"You shouldn't be so burdened," I put in.

Often through the years, and always at Christmastime when I reread the ballads, "Adoration," "Mary" and "The Pilgrim and the Fir Tree," I think of Byron's answer. I've heard other people quote the Lincoln story since then, but it was the first time I had heard it and I'll always associate it with the lanky young poet with calloused farmer's hands and a mind "thicketed" with beauty.

"Did you ever hear the Abraham Lincoln

story about the little boy he saw carrying a load on his back?" he asked. "Somebody said, 'Son, you've got a heavy burden there.' And the little boy replied, 'Sir, that ain't no burden, that's my brother.'"

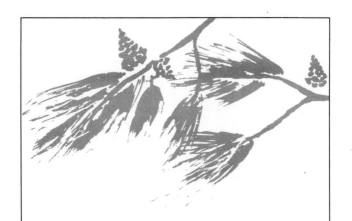

CHRISTMAS
IN CABBAGE
TOWN

SHE WAS CLIMBING BACK in her hospital bed when I went in and I offered her a boost.

"Okay," she said, "hold your arm there where I can lean on it."

I did and she glanced over her shoulder and smiled on me with great good humor.

"They told you I was going to die, didn't they?"

I nodded. Somehow, I guess I had known that if Sister Henrietta Keel ever died she would be radiantly pleased at the prospect. That final trip, as with all her lesser ones, would make her, in the old-fashioned phrase, journey proud.

She *was* journey proud. She had cancer and she didn't shy away from saying it. They operated and they told her it was too late. She was to stay in the hospital long enough to get her strength back and her stitches out and then go home and do anything she felt like doing.

She had plans and she wanted to talk about them. For more than ten years I had been on the periphery of Sister Keel's plans and there didn't seem any chance she would be planless now.

It must have been November when I first met Sister Keel. I always associate getting ready for Christmas with her. Somebody told me about a plain, aging angel in common-sense shoes who gathered children around her for games and stories on a vacant lot in

Cabbage Town every afternoon, and I went to see her.

The wind blew hard and cold across the hard-packed earth of the corner lot. Two dozen youngsters from toddlers to teenagers raced across the scraggly grass, yelled shrilly from seesaws and slides, pummelled one another and engaged in a one-sided football game more spirited than it was skillful. In the midst of them stood a sturdy, vigorous-looking woman wearing a bright wool dress, a scarf on her graying head and an expression of sunny serenity on her wind-reddened face.

Seven years before, Henrietta Hollis Keel had gone to work in the nursery at the nearby textile mill, telling Bible stories to the children of millworkers and illustrating them with pictures on a big board. She noticed — as she talked one day in the fence-enclosed nursery play yard — that an even bigger crowd of children had started gathering outside the fence to hear her. They came every day, ragged, barefoot, often dirty, and clustered against the fence listening.

"I asked myself, 'What am I doing in *here* with them out *there*'?" she related. "They need my stories worse than the children whose parents are working and who are eating regular!"

So Mrs. Keel resigned and set up shop on a vacant lot a few blocks away on Savannah Street and Pickett's Alley, in a grime-and-poverty-darkened neighborhood that was called "Cabbage Town" because cabbages kept its citizens alive during the depression.

The grief and the need Henrietta Keel saw around her, astonished her. She had lived a comfortable life, rearing her own four children in a pleasant house on a tree-lined street, with food and clothing sufficient to their needs. She hadn't really known that there were children in the same city who couldn't go to school or to Sunday school because they didn't have shoes to wear. She was appalled and heartsick when she found that little babies — who she loved with all her heart — were born every day into misery and want, with hardly a diaper to cover defenseless bottoms.

"I was ashamed of myself for what I had taken for granted," she remembered.

But Henrietta Keel, unlike most of us who are shamed by our complacency, did something her four grown-up children must have regarded as rather drastic. She took literally her Lord's admonition to sell all her goods and give to the poor and to take up her cross and follow Him. She sold her house, disposed of most of her furniture and moved into a tiny basement apartment which she wangled rent free.

From mill officials she begged the vacant lot and persuaded them to put a sturdy fence around it to keep the children safe from traffic. She got a farm bell to summon the children to play and she set out on foot in the neighborhood to get acquainted with the people.

The way she became known as "Sister" Keel in her nondenominational, unorganized church work was typical of her intuitive feeling about her new friends.

"This neighborhood is visited by a lot of social workers," she said. "Policemen, policewomen and truant officers are always coming and going. And they are all 'Miss' or 'Mister' or 'Mrs.' I wanted to be closer to these folks than that. I asked them to call me 'Sister Keel.'"

It was as if she had become blood kin to the residents of Cabbage Town. They took her to their hearts and she and the old farm bell became symbols of comfort and safety in a troubled world. She was there when the sheriff pitched their furniture onto the street, when the doctor wouldn't come, when a man went to jail and there was no grits or fatback for supper.

Living frugally herself, she begged from old friends and church groups so she could feed the hungry and clothe the naked.

Gradually, with the passage of time, help came. Young people's groups from churches pitched in to help her run the playground after school, to teach and direct. Churchwomen came and helped her run a vacation

Bible school in the summertime, sending teachers and, as she told me with a grin, "best of all — refreshments!"

First, she got a shed as a shelter from the winter wind and the blazing summer sun, grandly naming it the Haygood Memorial Methodist Shed for the church contributing the posts. Then the churchwomen began a campaign for funds for a little mission house.

With help, trouble inevitably came. Churchwomen made tours of the neighborhood to assess the need, and with them went newspaper reporters who saw the situation with ruthless objectivity, calling Savannah Street and Pickett's Alley a "slum" and reporting vividly its squalor.

Sister Keel's distress reflected the distress of some of the people up and down the street. They had pride and they loathed being objects of cool-eyed, bloodless charity. Some of them blamed Sister Keel and threatened to boycott the little mission house and to keep their children away from the playground.

"They are right," said Sister Keel sadly. "I

am one of them and I hurt when they hurt, but I brought in outsiders who didn't understand. I should have handled it differently."

To try to make amends, Sister Keel asked me to talk to some of the long-time residents of Cabbage Town and to publicize their points of view.

She introduced me to a slim young mother of four children, who was one of her helpers at the mission and who was angered by newspaper references to Cabbage Town as a slum.

"I tell them it's not the street that's a slum," Sister Keel said, smiling at the girl, her strong, gentle old face looking humorous and affectionate all at once. "The street is just earth like the good Lord put everywhere. We ourselves make a slum with the way we live."

The girl, Sylvia, nodded.

"I love this neighborhood," she said simply. "I know it don't look like much, but I was born here and my husband was born here and it's home to us. We moved away twice. We tried it in the project and the project apartments are nice and convenient. But I'm a hard person to get acquainted. Seems like I missed Savannah Street so much I could hardly stand it . . . so we came back."

Things were improving, Sylvia pointed out. Sister Keel had worked with the city and landlords to get minimal plumbing in the houses — not tubs or showers, of course, but water spigots and toilets. And the vacant lot where the children were playing bloomed now with the children themselves and the flowers which they and Sister Keel planted every spring. Sylvia remembered when it was just a catch-all for trash and junk "and all the men that got drunk would lie out here under a tree, cutting up and raising sand."

Sylvia was but one of the neighborhood women who worked with Sister Keel to change things and I was there in their moment of triumph. For weeks, Sister Keel had been collecting old clothes for a sale which Sylvia and some of her neighbors conducted. Good dresses and coats and little trousers were sold up and down the street for a few cents a garment. When the sale was completed,

Sylvia came in just as the churchwomen were canvassing the returns from their drive.

Sylvia held up her hand. "Cabbage Town," she cried, "gives $75!"

It was a triumph for Sister Keel, too.

"We have good people here," she said. "They'll make it."

The little mission was eventually finished and named Keel House over Sister Keel's protests.

"Ugliest name I ever heard of," she objected. "It doesn't mean anything. Name it Hope or Faith House — something that means something."

"Keel is another word for hope and faith," Sylvia said firmly, closing the matter.

Sister Keel loved Christmas and wherever she was, was somehow the Christmasiest place on earth. She started early every year with her sewing classes for young mothers and once I found her happily distributing materials for basketmaking.

"I want them to have something pretty in their homes that they made with their own

hands," she said. "To make something yourself and to be able to look at it and see its
beauty and see its flaws and think how you
would improve on it the next time . . . that's a
growing thing."

She had a warming, unabashed way of talking about poverty and happiness and God.
She could report a conversation with the
Lord as if He were the comfortable, under-
standing corner grocer and I always believed
every word of it.

There was the time when she decided she
was too old to climb around the roof of the
shed on the play yard, to put up the manger
scene which the men at the Union Mission
made for her.

"When it's up there in the yard, oh, it
brings a brightness to the whole street!" she
said. "I didn't see how I was going to get it up
and finally I told the Lord about it. I said,
'Lord, I want that manger scene out there but
You know I'm too old to put it up. Lord, is it
one of the things I ought to fold away and not
worry about?'"

The Lord, Sister Keel assured me, gave her an almost immediate answer. The phone rang and an Emory University theology student said he and a group of his friends wanted to offer their services to the mission for some Christmas chore. They were able-bodied young men who, he said, could "do anything."

"Can you put up a manger?" demanded Sister Keel quickly.

Sure, said the young man, and they'd give the mission a window washing and cleaning for good measure.

The students cleaned and the J.O.Y. Girls (Jesus-Others-and-You) were busy sewing away on Christmas surprises for their mothers. Another group of youngsters — who had been getting Saturday piano lessons from a volunteer music teacher — were rehearsing like mad for the community's first piano recital. All the other children practiced Christmas carols for the Cabbage Town Christmas party and Sister Keel stayed in a state of happiness very close to tears when she heard the little three-to-five-year-olds piping, "Away in de manger, No crib for He bed."

Eventually, Sister Keel moved on from Cabbage Town to Kelly Street to launch a new mission and that was the one she wanted to talk to me about at the hospital. She wasn't going to be able to stay with it long, her own strength wasn't what it had been, she said, but some of the churchwomen who had helped her on Savannah Street had transferred to the new Fellowship Mission and she spoke of them.

"Pretty soon now, they'll be making that Maytime check to see how many children will be starting to school next fall and helping them get ready. There's lots to do. New babies coming . . ."

Sister Keel's face softened and her eyes showed the first flicker of sadness. Death did not dismay her. She believed wholeheartedly in that "better place," but she hated to miss the arrival of one single new baby.

The day she left the hospital she summoned

me and all her "girls" at the mission to meet her there at eleven o'clock. She was going to the home of a relative in the country to rest a while and she wanted to commit the little mission and its charges to all of us — the women who had helped her so faithfully and to me as a sort of professional kibitzer.

"You don't have to write about it," she said, giving me a sharp warning glance. "God doesn't need any press agents for His work. But if my girls should need you, be there, won't you?"

Leaning on some of us, she walked around and looked at everything, pausing at an easel to pick up some cutout figures of Bible characters.

Her face glowed as she picked them up and lovingly smoothed and sorted the figures.

"When you tell this story to little children, keep it simple," she said.

And slowly, a little breathlessly, she began telling it, peopling it with the figures set on a felt-backed easel very like the one she had started out with in the mill yard.

There was a poor man who fell among thieves and was robbed and beaten and left by the roadside to die. A priest ("a preacher") and a Levite ("that's us . . . church members") came by and looked at the poor fellow and "passed on the other side."

Sister Keel paused when she came to that part of the story and her eyes moved over the faces around her.

"We have to be careful," she said gently, "that we don't do the same."

She finished the story and pretty soon her son came to take her away and we smiled and waved and called after her.

There are no monuments to Sister Keel. She died while a man I knew in Washington was trying to get her some kind of national award. (I was late getting the information to him because I dreaded a scolding from her. Public acclaim, she would have said, feeds no hungry children.)

But down on Kelly Street this Christmas, a gap-toothed little boy will sing:

CELESTINE SIBLEY

> *"I sing a song of the saints of God*
> *Faithful and brave and true ..."*

and all of us will think of Sister Keel, who did
not pass on the other side.

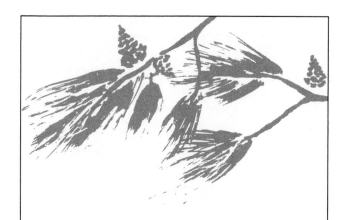

THINGS DON'T MAKE CHRISTMAS

THE LAST PERSON I HEARD speak of Things as if they had small importance in making Christmas was an old mountain friend in his late seventies. He came in to bring me some of those little red apples that are variously called Yates, lady apples and Christmas apples — small, ruby red and sweetly crisp.

He paused a while to speak of gifts and

givers.

"In a way, they didn't make much of Christmas when I was a young 'un," he said. "And in a way, they did. Ma and Pa didn't have cash money to spend on us, but they was about the givingest folks you ever saw."

"What kind of things did you get for Christmas?" I asked, hoping for a rundown on old-time play pretties and celebrations.

He chuckled.

"Once I got some copper-toed shoes. First I ever had that weren't homemade. About everything we had was homemade and we liked it fine. But the giving I'm talking about wasn't in Things."

And it wasn't just Christmas giving either, from the way he told it.

He shifted the basket of apples around and took one out and smoothed it on his heavy work jacket. What he said he had been saving to say, and it was important to him.

The things his parents gave him were all the knowledge they had — how to work for a living, how to "take a-holt" of an unhandy task, how to use themselves and the fields and forests around them.

"Pa thought learning us to work was worth every bit of time it took, even when he was pushed, and worth every mistake we made. Many a time I've seen him make me and the other bigger boys stand aside, while he let one of the little ones take his turn at learning something we could of done easy."

His parents gave him time — precious hours of listening when the children needed to talk.

"Ma did for a round dozen of us and I never once heard her say, 'Hush, run along, I'm busy.' She'd stand still with her hands in dough and listen bug-eyed to any fool thing we wanted to tell."

They gave him gaiety, fiddle tunes and ballads, and a joy in the natural things about him. They gave him religion. And they gave him a vision.

"Ma had a calendar a patent medicine salesman give her with pictures of Great Americans on it. She always thought every last one of us would be Great Americans."

He grinned.

"None of us ever got our pictures on a calendar that I know of. But I have a sister that's a missionary, three brothers that are preachers and one that's a doctor."

"And you?" I asked.

"I plant trees," he said with dignity. "Ma thought well of that."